THOMAS & FRIENDS

MOVIE THEATER
Storybook

based on *The Railway Series*
by The Reverend W Awdry

Track Trouble
Contents

Reader's
Digest
Children's Books®

Pleasantville, New York • Montréal, Québec • Bath, United Kingdom

Percy and the Carnival

DISK 1

1 On the Island of Sodor, children were waking up excited. The Sodor carnival was tonight! It would start with a big show of fireworks and a special visit from the Chinese Dragon. The children could hardly wait!

All of Sir Topham Hatt's engines were excited, too. They would bring all the rides and workers to the fairground for the carnival.

2 "I hope I get to pull the Chinese Dragon," puffed Percy.

Sir Topham Hatt arrived at Tidmouth Sheds to give the engines their jobs for the day.

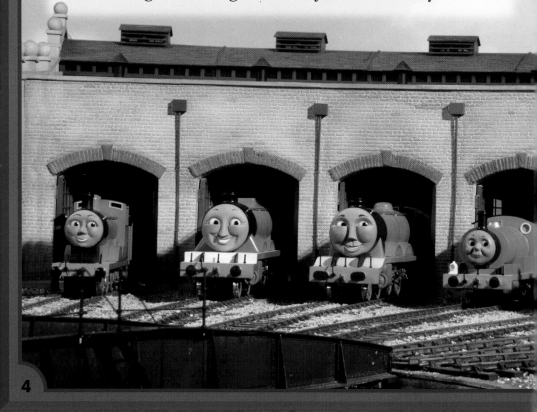

He asked Edward to pull the merry-go-round…Henry was to get the roller coaster…Gordon was to bring the workers to the fairground…Toby would collect the bumper cars…and Emily and James would fetch the Ferris wheel.

"And Thomas," boomed Sir Topham Hatt, "you are to collect fireworks as well as the Chinese Dragon."

Percy was disappointed. "What's my job, Sir?" he asked.

"You are to collect coal from the mines and fill the hoppers at all the stations," ordered Sir Topham Hatt.

"A railway can't run without coal," he added. "It's a very important job."

Then Sir Topham Hatt left. All the engines quickly chuffed off to work— all except Percy.

"Coal!" he huffed. Percy was very disappointed. He slowly made his way to the coal mines. Collecting coal didn't feel like a very important job at all.

"I wish I was pulling something exciting," grumbled Percy. "Not boring old cars full of coal!"

Percy gathered the freight cars and headed for the first station. He stopped at a signal that was near a school. Children were playing outside.

Just then, Toby puffed past pulling the bumper cars. When the children saw him, they began to clap and cheer!

Next, Edward came hurrying along the track. He was happily pulling the merry-go-round. The children cheered even louder.

"No one is cheering for me," Percy grumbled. "I knew pulling coal wasn't an important job."

Then Percy had an idea. "But helping my friends is important," he said happily. He left his coal cars behind and rushed off to find his friends.

Percy caught up to
Edward at a signal.
"Do you need any
help?" Percy wheeshed.
"No, thank you,"
said Edward. "I can
manage."
Just then, Toby
puffed by in a hurry.
Perhaps Toby needs some help,
thought Percy.
But Toby didn't need any help, either. "I will
need some coal soon," Toby told Percy. "That will
help me quite a bit."
But Percy wasn't paying attention because he
had just spotted James and Emily. He caught up
with the two engines at a crossing.

4

"That looks like fun!" tooted Percy. "But the big Ferris wheel must be very heavy. Would you like some help?"

"This is a big Ferris wheel," agreed Emily happily. "It's going to be the biggest ever!"

"But we don't need any help," added James as the crossing opened. "Even with a really big job like this."

Percy was feeling very upset. He saw Gordon pulling the fairground workers. Of course, Gordon didn't need any help. And neither did Henry, who was pulling the roller coaster.

Percy was not feeling very useful. All the other engines were working hard and having lots of fun. Then Percy saw Thomas waiting at the signal. Thomas was pulling the Chinese Dragon.

"Surely Thomas will let me help him," Percy said hopefully. But even Thomas didn't need any help.

"I am going to need some coal, though," said Thomas. "There was none at the last station."

Percy gasped. He had been so busy looking for other things to do, he hadn't delivered any coal yet!

As Percy hurried back, he saw Emily looking sad.

"There's no coal at any of the stations," Emily wheeshed. "None of us can get to the carnival."

"Cinders and ashes," cried Percy. "If the engines can't get to the fairgrounds, there won't be a carnival. All the children will be sad, and it will be all my fault."

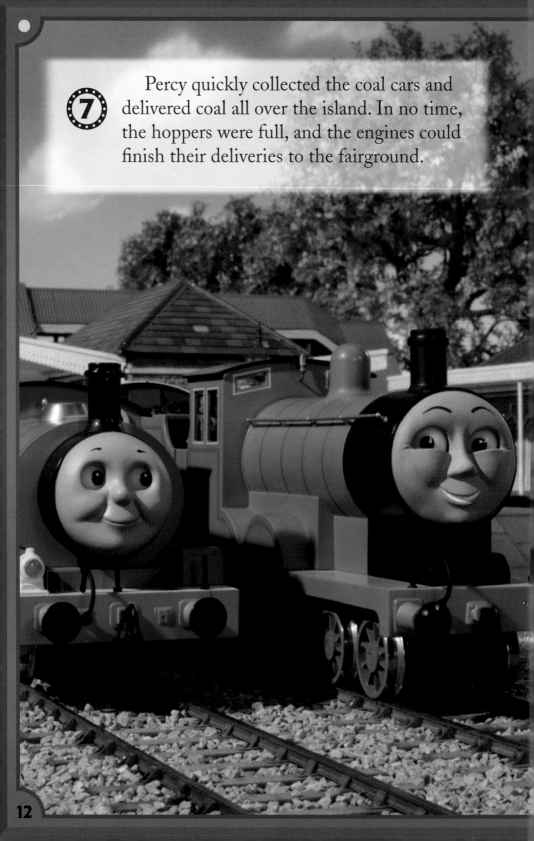

7 Percy quickly collected the coal cars and delivered coal all over the island. In no time, the hoppers were full, and the engines could finish their deliveries to the fairground.

Everything was ready just in time!

The sun was setting when Percy arrived at the carnival. Soon the fireworks began. Rockets soared into the air, the band began to play, and the Chinese Dragon danced!

The children cheered! And even though they weren't cheering for him, Percy was still very happy.

⑧ "I told you, Percy," Sir Topham Hatt said. "Delivering coal is a very important job."

Percy couldn't agree more.

Tram Trouble

DISK 1

1

One bright morning, Thomas puffed into the station at Arlesdale End. His good friend Toby the Steam Tram was there. Thomas was always happy to see his friend. Today he was even happier because Toby had some great news to share. Sir Topham Hatt had asked Toby to lead the parade at the very first Great Waterton Festival!

"That's because you are the only steam tram on Sodor," Thomas told his friend. "Everyone will cheer for you!" Toby looked a bit shy as Thomas said this, but his smile was as wide as ever.

Thomas puffed quickly on his way. Thomas had important work to do, and Sir Topham Hatt was waiting for him at Great Waterton.

Thomas didn't know it, but there was something else waiting at Great Waterton: a surprise!

As Thomas puffed into Great Waterton, he suddenly stopped. "Fizzling fireboxes!" he exclaimed.

There on the road next to the track was another steam tram! Sir Topham Hatt introduced her as Flora. "She is the new steam tram on Sodor," he informed Thomas. "Flora is to lead the parade with Toby."

Flora had a bright sunny smile, but Thomas had a hard time smiling back. "Toby thinks he's leading the parade all by himself," Thomas worried. "I must keep Flora away from Toby until after the parade." That would not be easy since Sir Topham Hatt had asked Thomas to take Flora to meet Toby. Instead Thomas took Flora to the Wood Yard. He thought if he delayed Flora, Toby would be gone by the time they arrived in Arlesdale End.

2

Flora dutifully followed Thomas as he set out to collect a flatbed of heavy logs at the Wood Yard. "Now we can meet Toby," he told Flora.

"Hooray!" she peeped in her pretty way.

Thomas felt the exact opposite. "Toby, Toby, you must go. Hurry now to lead the show!" he puffed to himself.

As they entered the junction to Toby's shed, it looked empty. Then Thomas saw a puff of steam! *Cinders and ashes!* he thought, screeching to a halt. Toby was in there after all. And Thomas couldn't let Toby see Flora.

"Quickly, Flora! I've just remembered," Thomas puffed. "We must go to the Docks first!" Flora was surprised, but she followed Thomas as he raced away.

At the Docks, Flora waited while Thomas picked up a large load that was completely hidden by a tarpaulin and rope. "Now we can meet Toby," Thomas told her.

Flora's sunny smile lit up the tracks. If only she had known what Thomas was really thinking. "Toby, Toby, please have gone. Lead the show! Be proud and strong!" Thomas said to himself.

Leaving the Docks with his large load, Thomas steamed strongly but Flora sadly chuffed to a stop. Following Thomas from place to place had used up all her coal. Thomas didn't think he could feel worse until he heard a chuff, and a puff, and the ring of Toby's bell. Now Toby had seen Flora! Flora had run out of coal! Neither would be at the parade. Sir Topham Hatt would be very cross.

To Thomas's surprise, Toby was very happy to meet Flora. "I was too scared to lead the parade all by myself," Toby confessed. "Now Flora and I can lead it togetther!"

Thomas knew he had to fix his mistake. He gave Flora his coal. "Now puff as fast as you can to Great Waterton!"

By the time Thomas got fresh coal and chuffed into Great Waterton, the parade was ready to start. But first Thomas's flatbed was unloaded. It was a wonderful new tramcar for Flora! Thomas proudly watched his two friends lead the first Great Waterton parade. He was so happy for Toby and Flora, and especially happy that his mistake hadn't spoiled the parade!

③
④

22